CRIMP

GENEVIEVE RAAS

RAVENWELL PRESS

Crimp:

Noun. A cleft stick attached to a spinning wheel,
used for holding the wool or flax the spinner will need.

Adjective. Of or concerning women.

THERE IS A misconception I would like to clear up, a misconception that has haunted your humble narrator for centuries.

It is the belief that villains are born.

I am here to tell you that is a malicious lie. Villains are *not* born. They are created, rising like twisted phoenixes from the ashes of humanity's betrayal. I should know. I am the result.

I have long been painted in a most unpleasant light. To some, I was a greasy goblin clawing for the fresh skin of a newborn. For others, I am an imp who tears himself in two as his name tumbles off the tongue of a queen.

Nothing could be further from the truth. Well, perhaps some is true, but that is an entirely different tale.

All you must know is I am not a hideous dwarf with an unkempt beard. I am actually quite tall and well-groomed. I may be pale, but I prefer to think that gives me a dramatic appearance. The one grain of truth to all the rumors about me is that I can indeed spin straw into gold.

I can also sense a desperate soul.

Did I forget to mention that? It is another one of those omissions and inaccuracies those two Grimm brothers seemed to delight in. It is much easier to frighten children with simplicity, and monsters are simple. Thus, the Grimms made me out to be a monster. Possibly I am. No, I am certain I am.

Yet, I wasn't always. I was made what I am.

A villain.

❧

"MY DAUGHTER IS coughing blood. She is at death's door," a withered old man pleaded. "That is why I come to you. They say you heal. No other reason I'd be in a gypsy camp if I didn't believe. Please, sir."

"You know the price," I said, negligently caressing the bottles in my case.

His face sunk further as he stared at the glass vials just beyond his reach.

"I have no gold for your elixirs," he stammered, meeting my gaze. "But, my daughter doesn't deserve such a gruesome death. She needs to be out dancing around the summer bonfires. She so loves to dance. Like a forest nymph, she is."

"I don't deserve to be short changed," I responded, eyes narrowing. These peasants always tried to get everything for free. But, everyone had a price they were willing to pay. The trick was to remain firm, cruel even, until they were broken.

"No, I suppose a man like you doesn't," he responded, surrendering with a sagging of his shoulders.

He patted around his jacket and pulled out quite the homely artifact. A shimmering chain of silver dangled from his gnarled finger. The small pendant hovered in the air waiting for my answer. The man's eyes were sunken and tired, but the flame of desperation I sensed blazed bright within his soul.

"Will you take my wife's necklace as payment instead?" he asked.

I suspected he took it without her consent.

Conceding, I took the pendant. A prettyish pattern was once etched across the surface, but years of anxious fingering had nearly rubbed it away. The necklace was nothing extraordinary.

"I take its value is only sentimental," I commented, letting the pendant swing back towards him.

"Please," the man cried. "To my wife, this necklace is worth far more than diamonds. I stand before you now offering you our greatest treasure in exchange for saving the life of our daughter."

He held the necklace out closer towards me. The man's despair was an inferno now. I hungered for it. Wanted it to be mine.

Before magic had poisoned me, I only saw sad faces and fearful eyes. Now, I tasted their anguish and drank the flames in their burning souls. I hungered for despair like the opium eater for the poppy.

"Alright," I said, taking the necklace and shoving it inside my jacket. "You have earned your daughter's life."

I pulled a small bottle from my case and infused the gin inside with a little dose of magic that would bring relief to her lungs. I handed it to the man.

"Take this vial, and when the moon is highest tonight, place four drops beneath her tongue. She will be dancing around the bonfire again in no time at all."

"Thank you, good sir!" he exclaimed, tears streaming down his leathery cheeks.

He grabbed my hand and started to shake it vigorously. I pulled it quickly away from him, hoping he didn't notice.

"What's that?" he asked, pointing at my now clenched fist. "Your palm is injured! You better get that stitched up before rot sets in and you lose it for good."

The man's loud voice caught the attention of one of the gypsy men, Zindelo. He looked in our direction, his large nose trying to sniff out any hint of sorcery. His favorite pastime fueled by his hatred of all things occult. If the camp knew what I had agreed to…what I was…I would have been strung up on the next tree as a demon.

Luckily, they believed me a charlatan like them. Selling snake oil to the fools who frequented their freak shows. As long as I didn't raise suspicion, I could maintain my small livelihood.

"It's nothing," I said, handing him his blue vial of liquid. A rush of satiation washed over me as his flame flowed into me through his gratitude. "Go on your way. I have more customers waiting."

"But sir…" he said, trying to reach for my hand again.

Zindelo took a few steps closer. I bristled.

I grabbed the man by the collar.

"If you say one more word I will take that bottle back," I hissed at him. "Now go. Or is your daughter not dying quick enough? Luck can change in the blink of an eye. Better be careful not to tempt it."

I released him and he almost stumbled backwards. The man's gaze widened in fear and he sunk away into the dark, his daughter's salvation clutched firmly in his hand.

I surreptitiously glanced around then breathed a sigh of relief. Zindelo was thankfully nowhere to be seen. I couldn't deal with any more close calls tonight. Shoving past the rest of my customers, leaving them to their fates, I crept back towards my tent.

The gypsy camp was beautiful at night. Their tents dotted the field and glowed like colorful paper lamps. Violins and drums cried out in wild notes that rose from around the campfires. It made my heart want to leap about in a savage dance.

On the way to my tent, I passed a group of horses, their dark hair glistening in the glow of the fire. Their tails whipped back and forth in agitation, but it was nothing to the loud whinnies that escaped their mouths as I passed them by.

Mehrewww!

Their hooves struck the ground, clouds of dirt rising up from the earth. Their nostrils flared knowing what I was. This was not an unusual reaction for them, but I decided to try for once to make them understand. I neared them and tried to stroke their noses to comfort them, but their eyes rolled back in their skulls as they shied away from me.

Mehrewww!

They stamped their hooves and thrashed against their ropes to avoid me. I walked away, swearing I would never go near them again. Animals were innocent, and I did not wish horror upon the innocent. The only animal I wished harm upon was the one man who drove me to become what I was now. The king.

I reached the safety of my tent and lit the small lamp. The bold reds and purples of satin and silk cushions and blankets came to life. I poured myself a glass of wine and drank it down. It burned my throat to guzzle it so quickly, but the rush of warmth was worth the price.

I fell back onto a pillow in a peaceful daze.

Was my hand that noticeable now? It would only be a matter of time before those superstitious fools would find out. But, I couldn't just leave. I was an outcast. If I ever showed my face in the kingdom again, I would be killed instantly for being born with the name Rumpelstiltskin. I was a man with little choice other than patience.

Slowly I turned over my hand. I cringed as I forced myself to look on the results of the choice I had made.

A scar. A long, jagged scar ran from the top of my palm to the base. The flesh was cut deep, nearly through to the other side of my hand. The marled skin was flayed on either side. It appeared freshly injured, but the truth was far darker.

This scar was the key to my revenge. It was where magic had entered my veins. Hopefully it would soon allow me the vengeance I sought.

The magic within me was growing stronger by the day, but it was still unrefined. More accurately, uncontrolled. I feared moments of anger. That is when it would burst out of me without warning. Zindelo waited eagerly for such a moment. I had to make sure that moment never came.

I grabbed one of the bottles strewn on the floor. I was growing bored with only being able to conjure these simple potions. If I wanted my revenge, I had to practice and do more than save peasants from disease.

Grasping it firmly I imagined the bottle morphing shape. The bulbous bottom grew, while the slender top twisted and shortened. The clear glass turned a bright shade of green. The texture was no longer smooth, but waxy. It gave slightly beneath my fingertips. My heart raced seeing a perfect apple in my hand.

My moment of triumph did not last long.

A crack echoed out. A split fractured down from stem to base. Shards of green fell to the ground like glass. It was glass.

What remained I threw across the tent, the echoing shatter mocking my failure. I was growing tired of patience.

I poured myself another cup of wine.

THE MORNING AIR was crisp and cool. Perfect weather for the labor of tearing down the camp and packing it away. Tents were rolled and neatly folded. Possessions were stowed in wagons and carts. In the blink of an eye, the field was restored to nature's rule as if we never existed.

"Here's a horse," Tobar said, pulling on the reins. The animal tugged back, whinnying loudly. "Still, girl! Best be careful, she seems to have gone a bit wild all of a sudden-like."

The horse reared, and the whites of its eyes shone like

slivers of the moon. Her tail whipped across its backside. Tobar yanked on the bridle, forcing the animal back down.

I took a step back not wanting to create anymore stress for the poor beast.

"It's no matter," I said, continuing to retreat. "I think I much rather walk. I could do with a little exercise."

"Rheinfelden is a whole days journey!" the man exclaimed. "You'll be left with only bloody stumps."

The horse tugged at him again.

"Then it's good I'm not wearing my good shoes. Wouldn't want them stained," I replied.

The man shook his head and turned away. The horse now clopped happily by his side.

The camp started their journey north. The horses trotted cheerfully ahead as I stayed far behind. The first half of the day was pleasant. But as the road grew rough and uneven, so did the blisters blooming on my feet.

I watched the pretty girl riding up ahead. I had seen her many times around the camp without paying her much heed. Dallying with women didn't interest me. Revenge was a fascinating but demanding mistress. But as a distraction from jabs of pain in my feet, the girl would serve.

Her flowing black hair shone in the sun as she combed her slender fingers through the strands. She gathered them in three thick ropes and folded one over the other. Then, she let the braid lose and the ropes spilled out back across her shoulders. I had to admit it was enchanting.

"I'd get my mind away from those thoughts you are having," Zindelo warned, slinking up alongside me. "Her father will flay you wide open and feed your guts to his dogs."

Zindelo circled me on his horse. He was fat and sweaty, his skin creased with dirt and tobacco.

"I was admiring the steed, not the girl," I lied.

"So you fancy an animal over the sweetness of a woman?" he taunted.

"I thought that loving livestock was your preference," I retorted.

"You pale bastard," he seethed. "No woman would ever want you. Everlida would as soon lie with a ghost from the grave as lie with you."

Magic stung my fingertips. Energy prickled over my skin. I forced a calming breath into my lungs, trying to quell my festering anger.

"I insult you, and you won't fight for your honor?" he laughed. "It's as I thought. You aren't a man. You are the dung beneath my boot."

The energy pounded up into my heart now. It vibrated my veins and shook through every muscle and tendon. There was no holding it back. It wanted out. It wanted vengeance.

The clasps of the cinch strap began to slip its buckles. His horse whinnied loudly and reared on its hind legs. In one great crack, the saddle slid off the horse, and Zindelo slid with it, landing with a nasty thump. Dust and gravel covered his hair, and blood rolled down his cheek.

I pressed my lips together trying not to laugh.

"You," he seethed. "You did this."

"I made you eat all those pastries and become obese?" I mocked. "It's a miracle your saddle lasted as long as it did."

He glared at me. Murder was written across his ugly face.

"I know you did this," he said, pointing a trembling finger at me. "I don't know how, but you did. I cinched that saddle myself. No way it broke without..." he whispered now, "sorcery."

"I think you hit your head a bit too hard with that fall," I said. "You were never clever, but now you've become fanciful."

Without a word, he got up and dusted himself off. He

replaced the saddle and remounted his horse. He struck its hindquarters with a good slap and rode off to the front of the group.

I breathed a sigh of relief, but I knew it was only a short reprieve. Zindelo was an idiot, but he was a persistent idiot, and those were always the most dangerous.

❦

THAT NIGHT WE entered the outskirts of Rheinfelden. The tents blossomed once more over the fields like enchanted mushrooms. The fortuneteller cleansed her crystal ball, and the bearded lady gave herself a quick trim to prepare for the night's first performance.

I kept far away as I readied my bottles for the desperate.

Two dozen different vials filled my stand. Taking a jug of cheap gin and jug of water, I filled each one carefully. Beside me sat different jars containing herbs and plants. I dug my hand into them and retrieved the dried herbs and plants I desired. Mugwort, chamomile, nightshade. All acted as the perfect conductor for my beginning magic.

Dropping them into the water, I stoppered the bottles and gave each a shake. The same energy I experienced earlier pulsated again, though at a lower frequency. A slight hum rose from the glass. The contents glowed dimly, the magic pulled from my force now suspended in the potion.

"Got anything to ward off the devil?" a gruff voice asked behind me.

I spun around.

Zindelo.

I looked up and saw him with several of his companions. They reeked of whiskey and horse dung. My nose stung from the stench. Their eyes shone brightly against their tan and dirty skin. Sweat stained their graying shirts.

"Apparently not, as I haven't been able to keep you away," I hissed. "All I have are water and plants."

His friends snickered. Zindeldo put up a silencing hand and a hard hush fell over them.

"Water and plants, you say?" he asked, picking up one of the vials. "I doubt that."

He threw it against the table and clear pebbles exploded over the wooden surface.

"What are you doing?" I yelled, stilling his arm before he threw another.

"Ridding the world of your devilry!" he screamed. "I've been watching you! The rumors are true – you're the Devil himself!"

He smiled revealing a set of rotting teeth. His breath stank worse than himself and I turned my head as far as I could. Then I saw what he truly intended. His friends brought out hefty sticks and small clubs, tapping them against their palms. My heart pounded as anger ate at me.

"I followed that man yesterday," he continued. "The one with the dying daughter. The moment the liquid touched her lips her eyes shot open. Her coughing stopped, and she stood as swiftly as if it were morning. Water," he drawled out the word, "wouldn't do that."

I saw the flash of a blade as he pulled it from his pocket.

"Why are you upset that a girl has her life back?" I argued, grasping desperately at the last threads of my composure. "Miracles can happen, you know. Maybe it was God's will. The rest is coincidence."

"It was the Devil's will!" He shouted. "*Necromancy*."

He flipped my table, cracking the wood and sending the bottles crashing. I looked from the shattered glass to the men that surrounded me now. Their glazes spoke plainly of their wish to see me bleed.

"You used to be a good chap," Zindelo said. "A fake and a

liar, sure, but you weren't tainted. The last several months I've watched you change. Animals fear you. There's a darkness over you. A shadow. I can feel it. We all can feel it. A black energy suckling away at us like the Devil at a teat."

Quicker than I could react he grabbed my wrist and peeled open my fingers. The proof of what he said quivered with every beat of my heart. The scar betrayed what I was.

"Heaven save us," Zindelo gasped. "You made a pact with—"

"Yes!" I snapped. "I made a deal. A bargain. I would do it all again to get what I truly want, something a man like you would never have the courage to do."

Zindelo let go of me as if I were diseased. The men backed away, nearly stumbling over one another.

I spread out my arms, enjoying the fear I was generating in them. The force rattled through my core and the heat built up in the palms of my hands. Confidence as I'd never known flourished as I saw I could squish them all like bugs.

"The only question now is, what are you going to do about it?" I asked almost cheerfully. "I have magic, and you have nothing but your dim wits."

One man screamed, another crossed himself. Neither had any effect on me besides amusement. I approached them, the energy screaming through my veins now pounding in my fingers. A bright glow radiated from my palms and illuminated their horrified faces.

I laughed as I raised my hands, palms out, and pushed the lustrous orb against them. The light sprung from me and leapt towards their trembling forms. Like a wave, it rolled full and strong, then grew thin until it flickered and went out entirely.

The energy in my bones dissolved, leaving me limp and dismayed.

I begged it to return, but it remained deaf and dead. I was

utterly defenseless. The men, for all their dim wits, quickly realized this. Their prayers for mercy turned into mocking laughter.

"He's a farce!" one said, daring a step closer.

"Let's end this," Zindelo commanded, grabbing a stick.

I started to run. I didn't get very far.

Pain shot through my skull and a loud crack echoed in my ears. The rush of blood and the beating of my heart filled my hearing. Through the haze I stumbled, but regained my footing. Sounds cleared, even if my sight remained dark.

Another strike. Another flash of pain. It rippled over my brain and down my neck like lightning. Everything blurred. I was on the ground. I grasped at the grass and dug my knees into the dirt, trying to drag myself away from them. A foot pressed down against my cheek. Earth filled my nose and the metallic taste of blood my mouth.

Shots of agony hit my sides and stomach as something hard slid into my flesh. Warm liquid gushed over my skin. I flailed as a foot kicked me in the gut. Bones cracked, and my chest throbbed. I couldn't breathe. I gagged on blood now, but they didn't relent. Another strike to my head and I screamed out, bursts of light flashing in my vision.

"Stop!" I gurgled.

Their laughter bled through the beating of my heart.

I was dying. Well, my body was dying. My soul wanted to leave the agony it was suffering behind. It yearned for the heaven it had been promised since a small child. The magic that made me an immortal now prevented my soul from reaching what it desired. I was trapped. A force like a metal cage surrounded my body. My soul pounded against it, but it didn't budge. I was entombed inside this hell forever.

I focused all my strength on opening my eyes, but they wouldn't. My fingers next. I tried to concentrate on the sensation of them pulsing, but they couldn't move. I was paralyzed, dead to the world but to myself.

"What should we do with the body?" a man asked.

"We could chop him up and feed him to the dogs," another suggested.

I prayed for anything but that. I would be nothing but a rolling head, consumed by the gnashing teeth of a dog.

"Wouldn't do to poison the dogs," Zindelo's greasy voice guffawed. "We throw him in the river. No one is going to care who killed him. Hell, we'd probably get a medal for saving the crown the trouble of burning such a foul beast."

Their hands wrapped around my wrists and ankles. I wanted to scream out as my broken bones scrapped against one another, but my voice was silenced. My body was dead and the magic I so desired now trapped my soul within. Fear rippled through me. What if my body never healed? Would I be a living soul trapped inside a bloated corpse forever?

Rushing water thundered beside me. My body swayed, my bones cracking with each movement. Then I was falling. Falling until cold water splashed over me. It entered every cut and filled my lungs until they burned.

Still I didn't die, though I wished for nothing more.

Rocks pelted my head and arms. Darkness and cold consumed me. Then, there was nothing.

❧

I DON'T KNOW how long I tumbled through the river. My body was absolutely frigid, numbing cold replacing the pain. The rough waves grew calm and I rose to the surface. Soft water lapped against my cheeks and trickled into my nose. Light flooded the darkness of my still closed eyes.

A hard surface came up beneath me rescuing me from the

current. I was finally still, though my legs continued to float in the chill. What parts of me were exposed to the sun began to thaw. Warmth seeped through my skin and into my bones. My cuts once again began to sting.

My blood vibrated. My eyes shot open. I was staring at the sky. White clouds floated above and branches filled with green leaves rustled prettily.

My fingers could wiggle. So could my toes. I was being restored, life regenerating my dead flesh. I should have died the moment the first strike broke my skull, but I survived. Truly, my magic was more powerful than I had ever imagined.

Or, perhaps I was a monster, after all.

A pressure grew in my chest. It bore down on my lungs and stomach, the spasm sending water pouring out of my mouth. My lungs were clear, and fresh air filled them with healing breath. I cleared my throat, flinching as the tendons in my neck snapped and popped.

My pulse quickened. Someone heard me. I wasn't alone.

I sensed a flame nearby. It came closer. I could see the little orb move through the fields. It neared the waters edge.

It saw me. A soul in need of something I somehow desperately wanted to give.

I looked up and the face of a young woman peered down at me. Her arms dropped the linens and paddles she had brought for washing. Shock forced her mouth to open, but she didn't scream as I expected. Racing down the bank, her bare feet squelching in the mud. Without a care for her skirts, she fell to her knees beside me in the brackish dirt. With trembling hands, she gently touched my broken body.

"Help," I rasped.

She fell backwards, the sludge squishing beneath her. She obviously had believed I was dead. Regaining her composure, she scrambled back to me. Her lips were pink and cheeks rosy. The sun illuminated her blonde hair causing her to resemble a gilded icon in a church. She was an angel fallen from heaven, and I a demon spat out of hell.

"Help," I slurred again.

She stood and put out a finger motioning me to wait. My blood already stained her apron, but she didn't seem to care. She hiked up her skirts and ran back up the hill leaving me alone.

Though out of sight, I could still follow her flame as it sprinted across the fields, as it entered a barn, as it ran back towards the bank where it desired to help me. I didn't know why it bothered, but I was too weak to think much, let alone argue the moral politics of redemption.

She slid back down the bank and spread open a large linen sheet beside me. She placed her hands beneath one side of my body. She was warm against my frigid skin, and I savored the contact.

I gasped in pain as she rolled my body onto the sheet. My breaths quickened and my face scrunched together as I waited for the wave to pass. She cupped my cheek in her hand, her eyes full of apology. I looked away, unsure what to do.

As my breathing grew even, she grabbed the two ends of the sheet and pulled me up the bank. She huffed and her eyes only grew brighter from the exertion. I cursed myself for having turned away from them. I was like a child. Terrified of what it didn't know.

A cow moaned.

Moouugh! It wailed, just as the horses had screamed.

She looked it in the eyes and stroked its cheek. Her gentle touch calmed the beast enough to be reconciled to carrying a monster. I don't know how she managed it, but she dragged me onto the cart.

The cart began to move and I was jostled back and forth.

Each bump was agony. Either my head wanted to split like an egg or my stomach wanted to vomit from the excruciating sensations rippling over me. The hard wood pushed into my broken bones, and I screamed.

I concentrated on the clouds floating slowly past as we moved through the field. For a moment, I was floating with them. The woman was by my side.

SHE PLACED ME atop a straw mat on the wooden floor of her cottage. Dried herbs hung from the rafters. A fire burned low in the hearth, a pot of stew by the smell of it simmering away. Another pot sat on the hob, water heating inside it. The only thing out of place was the glass figurine of a swan. It sat on the mantel, its delicate beauty a stark contrast to the surrounding rustic simplicity.

She placed a collection of ceramic pots and a trivet on the ground. A small pile of torn rags appeared by my head. She took the pot of water from the hob and set it on the trivet, then knelt down by my shoulders.

"Who…are you?" I pushed out. I ignored the cracking and bleeding of my lips as they formed words.

She didn't answer, only placed her hot finger against my bloody lips. I understood. It was time to be quiet.

She slowly untied my shirt. The laces slipped through her fingers easily enough, but dried blood acted as an adhesive between the fabric and my skin. I hissed as she peeled the shirt from my chest, the material ripping the tender scabs.

She gasped and covered her mouth in shock. Tears swam in her eyes, even as she shook her head in disbelief. I looked down. Black and blue welts covered me like a grim leopard. Deep gashes cut into my flesh, barely masked by sad scabs. My left arm was bent unnaturally.

She breathed deeply as if preparing for what more was to come.

She blushed with charming innocence as she slid my trousers down past my hips. Rose was quickly replaced by white as she saw my twisted leg. A sliver of bone stuck out of the skin, the flesh around it infected and inflamed.

Rage filled me at seeing the results of Zindelo and his cronies. They made me a mangled corpse. Now, I was left to wander eternity as a freakish cripple.

She dipped a cloth in the hot water and gently sponged my skin. I grumbled and grit my teeth. She gripped my hand, and my eyes snapped to the connection. Our hands were folded one within the other. I looked at her and saw a reassuring smile on her lips.

I was frozen with feeling too much and nothing at all.

She squeezed and dipped her chin as if asking permission to continue. I managed a small nod, daring to squeeze her hand in return.

I held my breath as the steaming material slid down my chest and over my stomach. She cleansed my wounds, but little did she know she also scrubbed my spirit clean. As her cloth swept away hardened blood, her kindness removed my heart's scarring, layer by layer, and I was powerless to stop it.

Clouds of crimson blossomed in the water as she rinsed the cloth. Moving on to my arm and leg, she carefully washed around the broken bones.

I hated what would come next.

She twisted a clean rag into a rope and placed it between my teeth. My breathing deepened though it hurt my bruised ribs. She didn't look at me now. Wouldn't. Her soul told me she hated causing pain, even if it was necessary.

Furrowing her brow, she held my arm between both her hands. A quick twist and pop, and fiery agony flooded my arm. I bit down hard against the cloth, my scream muffled. My bone was set.

She then turned to my crooked leg. Holding it in the same fashion, she felt first for the correct points. Still refusing to meet my gaze, she gripped above my ankle and pulled my leg. I nearly swallowed the cloth as my mouth opened in an awful scream. The bone went back beneath the skin, and a disgusting snap told us it was back in its rightful place.

Sweat ran down into my eyes, mingling with my tears. My stomach roiled. A warm hand wiped away the wet droplets. Our eyes met, and I'd never seen such a sorrowful gaze. I was too exhausted to speak, but I slowly closed and opened my lids letting her know all was well. I may have thrived on guilt and despair, but I did not want hers.

She opened her collection of little pots and dug her fingers into the thick oils and creams, rubbing them over my wounds and gashes. The sting was bearable, especially if I focused on the sensation of her touch. When I was made an outcast as a child, I encountered only hatred and a kick or a slap. This was the first time someone touched me willingly.

Lovingly.

I savored each precious moment that slipped by.

She took long strips of cloth and wrapped them around me, covering my wounds and swathing the splints of my arm and leg. When she was done, she offered me food. I eagerly accepted.

She fed me spoonfuls of warm, savory potage. Bits of barley and beef mingled enticingly together on my tongue.

With each bite, I could sense my strength returning. I wanted to believe it was due to her help, but I knew it was the magic in my veins. I had practically risen from the dead in a matter of hours. There was no saying how fast my bones and wounds would heal now I had received such tender care.

I only hoped it wasn't too quickly to cause her concern,

or worse, to realize what I was. But as she spooned another mouthful of stew between my lips, I found I didn't care. I only wanted this moment to last forever. To feel cared for. Wanted.

Once the bowl was empty, she covered me in a blanket and stroked my hair. The fire lit her from behind just as the sun had earlier in the day. Her curls shone so brightly they resembled a crown of gold. There was nothing she deserved more than to be a queen.

However, there was something unsettled about her. She was beautiful and seemed to lead a simple life, yet, she was troubled. The flame in her soul craved something desperately, but I didn't know what. It glowed brilliantly in her chest wanting me to fix it.

I was bewitched.

I stretched out my arm trying to touch the golden orb. My fingers almost touched the soft flesh above where it hovered when she grabbed my hand and placed it back at my side. Confusion danced across her gaze, though she didn't speak out against my sudden break in etiquette.

"Sorry," I rasped out. "I was overcome by…"

I stopped speaking. What could I say? *I felt your soul?* That would surely scare the poor creature. That was the last thing I wanted.

Silence tented over us, only the crackle and spit of the fire daring to make a sound.

N IGHT CAME, AND I fell away to dream.

There I stood atop a hill. Whole. Pure. Untainted.

The scar on my hand didn't exist, and my blood flowed through my veins smooth and untroubled by hate.

There was only myself and the Angel with her golden curls. We stood side by side high on a hill staring down at the town below. The sun warmed our skin, and darkness was half a world away.

We were free.

Cookakew!

The vision shook, then crumbled. The Angel was swept up by the sky. I was swallowed by the earth.

Cookakew!

My eyes shot open. The first pale rays of light beamed through the open window.

"Damn rooster," I thought, rubbing my eyes. I cringed forgetting the cuts and scrapes all over my face.

As I feared, my broken arm and leg were nowhere near as sore as the day before, though they were still more than painful enough. My lungs could easily fill with deep breaths. My torso didn't feel it would tear if I moved or twisted to quickly.

I grunted as I forced myself to sit up. I looked down at my chest. The map of bruises was already fading. The cuts were more shallow scratches than the deep gashes of mere hours ago. Only the scar on my hand remained unaltered.

I heard footsteps coming down the stairs. I laid back down and pulled the cover over my body. I cringed, dreading what she would think when she saw such marked improvement in one night. She would know I wasn't fully human. Then, she would scream and kick me out to the streets.

Through slitted eyes, I watched as she gracefully moved about the room building the fire back up from the night. She poured a bowl of grain and water into the pot. Within moments, I smelled porridge beginning to simmer over the fire.

I prayed she would believe me still asleep, but my stomach betrayed me rumbling in hunger.

Her skirts dusted the floor as she approached. She knelt beside me and smiled. I gripped the blanket wishing to hide the truth, but where I could withstand strength, her softness undid me. She gently coaxed my hands away and pulled it back.

She traced the bandages, inspecting which needed changing. She slipped her fingers under the edge of the bandage that was wrapped around my chest and tried to look underneath.

"Hungry," I yelped.

She startled and lost her balance, rocking back on her heels then plopping down on her bum. At least her fingers had let go of the bandage. Behind my weak smile of amusement, I breathed a sigh of relief. She hadn't seen.

She smiled at her silliness and went to bring me a bowl of porridge. I was touched by the way she added fresh cream and brown sugar when she could have saved her supplies and given me the plainest of gruels. The porridge warmed me from within, but her kindness fed another, older hunger within me.

"What is your name," I asked, once the bowl was finished.

She remained silent, though her flame oddly began to blaze again. A deep sadness shadowed her features. She abruptly stood and took the bowl away.

"You don't have to be afraid to tell me," I said after her.

She placed the bowl on the table and remained still with her back against me.

"You have done so much for me," I continued. "I have not known such kindness in years. I owe you everything. You must tell me your name, if only that I may bless it."

Silence answered me, though her soul continued to smolder. It called to me, begged me, but I couldn't for the life of me understand what it wanted. All I knew is I would give it whatever it desired. If I had not already lost my soul, I would have given it to her with my heart.

A knock at the door caused us both to jump. Alarmed, I

watched her answer the door and admit a powerfully-built man carrying two jugs.

"Brought in the milk," he said, walking in as if it was his own house. "That cow is such an aggravating creature. If she doesn't stop trying to kick over the bucket, she's going straight into the pot."

She rolled her eyes at him and smirked. He laughed as he put the pitchers on the table then wrapped his hands around her waist.

The brazen bastard! Who was he to touch her, to smutch her with his hands? Something hot and sick shot through my blood.

He looked at me, and I returned the favor of scrutiny.

He was young and brawny. His white blonde hair and brown skin no doubt came from the fields he obviously worked in, as did the mud on his boots. I could see from his open countenance that the fool understood little past the simple life of a farmer. Otherwise, he'd have been more wary at the sight of one such as I.

He came over and crouched down, looking me over like one of his prized hogs. I tensed, wanting to test my magic by turning him into a hog.

"He doesn't look half so bad as you described, Clarice," he said. "You acted like you thought he was dying. Looks like he took a bad fall from his horse is all."

He prodded my shoulder, and I hissed as pain throbbed down my arm and back.

"Watch it," I seethed.

"Beg pardon," he said, smiling apologetically. "I don't mean any harm. She acted like you were about to kick the bucket last night. I shouldn't be surprised, though. It's hard understanding her sometimes. You wouldn't believe the misunderstandings we've had."

"Misunderstandings?" I questioned, curious.

"Surely you noticed?" he asked. "She's mute. Can't say a thing. Her hearings just fine, but not a word has ever passed her lips. I'm Marcus, by the way."

I looked at Clarice kneading dough, her chin down and avoiding our gazes. Her flame was an inferno now, and I finally understood.

She wanted to speak. She wanted me to give her a voice.

"That's all old news, though," Marcus said. "The news I want to know is who are you? Is there anyone we can send a message to for you?"

He sat down in the chair near my cot and took a bite out of the apple he had pulled from his pocket.

"I'm no one," I said.

"No one?" he chuckled. "That doesn't seem to be the case to me. A 'no one' usually doesn't get beaten within an inch of their lives and thrown in a river. No, you are definitely a *someone* to make anybody that angry."

He took another bite of his fruit, his lips smacking disgustingly together. I hated him.

Pop!

His apple exploded in his hand, juice dribbling down his fingers. My eyes widened, and I realized I had better get a grip before I made his head do the same as his fruit.

"Whoops!" he exclaimed then laughed. "Sometimes, I don't realize my own strength."

He picked up the larger broken bits off the floor and ate them one by one. I couldn't help my lips from twisting with revulsion. Perhaps turning him into a hog wouldn't be that much of a stretch after all.

"Tell me the truth," he said. "What's your name?"

He popped another dirtied piece of fruit in his mouth and sucked the juice off his thumb. I couldn't believe such a fool was interrogating me. At this point, I would tell him anything just to make him leave.

"I am Henry Fixwish," I lied. "I am a traveling apothecary heading north. Highwaymen fell upon me, taking everything. I was foolish to attempt reaching the next inn instead of stopping at sundown."

Marcus shook his head. "There are a great deal of thieves along the roads in these parts. It's tempting fate to travel after dark."

"It certainly is," I sighed, thinking of just how much temptation I had thrown fate's way the past few days. "Suffice it to say, if it wasn't for…Clarice… I'd most certainly be dead in a ditch, quite literally."

He smiled broadly and gazed at her in a way that was too complacent with her kindness, as if he expected no less from her. Did he not know what a rare treasure her compassion was? A muscle tic twitched at the corner of my left eye.

My skin prickled with a rush of energy. Even the hairs on my arms stood on end. The magic within me wanted to lash out.

I took a deep breath trying to contain it, otherwise I would take him well past a hog and serve him up as bacon on my plate.

"She is an angel," he praised casually. "Always taking care of injured kittens or motherless squirrels. You can always count on if anything is battered, she'll be nursing it back to health."

He got up from his chair and walked to her. Pink danced in her cheeks as he leaned in and whispered something in her ear. His hand lingered on her lower back, his fingers twirling in a circle.

Magic thundered in my soul. It sparked and thrashed in my blood. My hands trembled.

I tried to breathe again…

CRACK!

Glass shattered, and white splinters snowed on the floor.

A round fragment rolled over to me. Looking down, I saw the head of the swan figurine rocking and wobbling.

Clarice clapped both hands over her mouth. She tried to pick up the pieces of the disintegrated bird with trembling fingers. A tear skated down her cheek.

I cursed myself for letting a bit of jealousy destroy something so special to her. I learned long ago the sentimental always had the greatest value to a soul. Now, I had robbed her of the only thing that ever meant anything to her.

Marcus crouched behind her and placed his hand on her shoulder.

"It's ok, Clarice," he said soothingly. "I know it was the last possession of your mother's, but it's only glass. The broken pieces can't break your memories."

She threw him off at this and stomped over to the shelves, rummaging until she found a small jar. Reverently, she placed the pieces into it as if she was handling the bones of a saint.

I covered my head with the blanket like a child, too ashamed by what I had allowed my emotions to cause to keep looking...afraid if I continued to watch Marcus touch her, I would only destroy everything, including the roof above our heads.

MARCUS LEFT SHORTLY after, though, not before he threatened to come back later in the evening and check in on my "progress." I was glad to be rid of him. I'm sure he wasn't thrilled about another man in the house, but I wasn't thrilled about his very existence. At least Clarice, my Angel, was all mine again for a few hours more.

My shame about the swan was replaced by a new anxiety.

Clarice was putting out the ointments and creams. She

cut fresh bandages in long strips and boiled water. The moment I dreaded approached.

My breathing grew shallow. My heartbeats pounded in my ears. What would she think of me when she saw how fast and how much I had healed?

I would have left if I could. My lacerations were sealing shut. But, the bones in my leg were not completely mended and would not bear my weight for a single step. I would be forced to see her face cloud in confusion before dissolving into disgust.

She began unwrapping the bandages from my torso then washed away what little blood still stained me. She stopped. I prepared for the worst.

Her fingers traced over my skin, and I shivered from the sensation. I searched for revulsion in her face, but I saw only wonder in her eyes. Our gazes locked, and she smiled slowly in relief. She pointed to my disappearing wounds and nodded happily. I could only stare at the tears of joy streaming down her face.

Clarice didn't care how quickly I was healing, only that I was healing. I wasn't hated as a freak or abhorred as a sinner. I was loved for exactly what I was.

She continued to wash my body and replace bandages. The entire time I could only marvel at such a wondrous creature. We were both different, cut off from the world in our different ways. Her being mute, and me, well…

However, when she unwrapped my hand, the wound was still just as fresh as ever. She stilled, but didn't recoil. Her fingers glided around the bewitched scar, noticing the odd elasticity covering it. Her eyes flickered from the scar to my face, and though mute, her question was clear.

A rush of honesty throbbed in my soul. It demanded to slip off my tongue. I ached to tell her the truth of what I was.

She tried to wash the blood frozen in time from my hand. She frowned as the scar remained stubbornly immovable.

I reached out and placed my hand atop hers. It was thrilling to touch another being. She didn't pull away. Her pulse beat excitedly beneath my palm. I savored every precious one, praying they beat for me.

"You want to know about this wound?" I asked.

She nodded her head, inching closer. Her fingers gripped my hand. I thought I would be undone.

"It's not a wound. It's a scar," I said, struggling to compose myself.

She raised her brow in surprise.

"I know it is hard to believe, but when I tell you, you will understand," I said. I inhaled deeply, ignoring a rush of anxious dizziness. "I was not robbed. I am not a lone traveler. My name isn't Henry Fixwish."

I spoke my true name aloud. She gasped. No doubt she had heard tales as a child of my vile family. I waited for her to pull her hand back, to remove it from such soiling contact.

She squeezed my hand and nodded solemnly instead. My hell had become a paradise.

"The king has cursed me and proclaimed me a traitor, and the king's word is law," I said. "But, the king's word is not truth. His words are lies spelled with bloody letters and spoken in tones of greed. The truth is that he burned my heart to ash, leaving nothing but smoke and death to fill the emptiness."

I took a deep breath to calm the bitter magic that stirred in my veins.

"A man without a heart is nothing more than a monster. He may have created me, but I know well enough that I am more a monster from the choices that I must now make."

She cupped my face and shook her head. I pressed her

hand into my cheek wanting to believe her, but I let it fall away.

"I am a monster," I persisted. "This scar proves it. I was offered magic for vengeance, and without a thought to consequence or virtue, I took it. I live now only for one purpose. Greed destroyed me, and by greed, my destroyer shall receive his reward." I paused, suddenly struck by the magnitude of what I had done. "I have never told anyone of this. You are the only one to know the truth of me, of my quest."

I searched her face for hatred, but all I found was concern, compassion, and even curiosity.

"Am I not abhorrent to you?" I asked.

She shook her head, her flame burning brighter. I swallowed hard. The magic was humming hard under my skin. She must have felt it somehow, for she startled a little and looked at our joined hands in wonder.

"Do you want me to show you?"

She nodded and smiled wide.

Closing my eyes, I released her and held out my hand. In my mind I saw a simple rose with a green stem and red petals. In my vision, I saw it blossom slowly and float over my outstretched fingers.

Magic made my palms itch, heating the blood beneath my scar. I prayed it was working and producing a rose and not, say, a skunk.

Daring a peek, I saw her awed face. The red rose really existed, floating just above my open palm. I allowed myself to breathe again.

Grasping it in one swoop, I held it out to her. She took it and buried her nose within the soft petals. Her flame glowed brighter than I had ever experienced with anyone. I swore I could almost hear whispers now. The words were faint and indistinguishable, but I knew now what they wanted.

"I can also sense a desperate soul," I murmured.

She looked up sharply from the rose, fixing her eyes on me. Her flame blazed. The whispers grew louder.

Let me speak, they chanted, the words as delicate as music but as determined as drums.

I reached out towards her fire.

Let me speak. Please, God, they shouted now, ringing in my head like great bells.

Her skin was fire as my fingertips grazed the area above her bosom. Euphoria stung my soul. I pressed more firmly. She didn't pull away, and I liked to imagine, she leaned toward me ever so slightly. I laid my hand fully over her chest, my fingers spreading across her exposed flesh. Her heart pounded into my palm, and I bit my lip, knowing mine now beat in time with it.

She trusted me. I trusted her.

She was crying. Tears like crystal rolled down cheeks and fell on my flesh, warm as a summer rain.

Let me speak! Give me a voice! her soul cried out.

There was nothing I craved more in that moment, or any moments since.

Closing my eyes as tight as I could, I envisioned a glowing, golden orb. Energy pulsed and built within my core. The ball hovered between us, hot and molten. Murmurs and whispers radiated from the round surface.

It was a voice. Her voice.

The orb began to spin. The magic poured out of me in torrents, but I continued on, drawing on every ounce of power I possessed. I moved the voice orb towards her lips. Her mouth opened as if to receive it. It spun faster, glowing brighter than before, the sounds louder and more sure.

My hands cramped in stabbing pangs, and my breath turned shallow as I sent more magic into the spell.

The orb flickered.

Fear seized me.

I cried out from the effort of forcing one last burst of magic into the spinning globe. The sphere flashed and flared like a flame in the wind before blinking out suddenly and completely.

I had failed.

I gasped for breath, struggling to comprehend the fact.

She wiped away a tear, and I knew it was the last one she would shed for me. She would hate me now.

"I'm sorry," I whispered. "I suppose monsters are not meant to heal."

She frowned, and anger blossomed red across her chest. I hung my head, ready to receive her wrath. How could she not be angry at me for leading her on?

Grabbing my scarred hand she peeled back my fingers revealing my sin. My hand trembled locked tightly in her grasp. I feared what she would do but I knew whatever it was I deserved it.

Soft heat blazed over the wound. I thought I would shatter. She was kissing my palm. Kissing! I was the one that had failed her. I led her to believe I could cure her, and here she was showing *me* mercy. In an instant, the crutches of anger holding up my soul were kicked away. I was undone.

Her lips trailed from the top of the scar to the bottom, a fire left in their wake. As tears now fell from both our eyes, I knew in that moment I would love her forever.

"I swear I will give you a voice," I whispered to her. "I will work until the earth is dust to grant your wish."

❧

WE WERE BONDED after that. Akin.

I resolved to savor that memory and keep it fresh in my mind until my dying day. I had been shown mercy in the simple form of a kiss. In the past, no one had so much as given me a scrap of bread, but this woman, she pressed her naked lips against the foulest part of my body and hadn't recoiled in disgust.

In the deepest recesses of my soul, I dared to believe she could love me.

Anytime she tended my healing bones and wounds, my heart fluttered for her. Even though I couldn't give her what she desired, she still always smiled and ran her fingers through my hair to try and tame its tangles. Her touch was its own kind of magic, and I couldn't imagine she felt differently.

I cursed myself that my magic was not strong enough to quell that flame smoldering within her soul. Once I mastered its full potential, whenever that day would be, I swore I would make her sing with the angels.

In the darkness of night, I practiced magic. I repaired the bowls she had cracked through the day. I swept the hearth of ashes without raising a finger. I was even able to heal the broken wing of her best goose. She had hugged me for that one. I would have mended a thousand goose wings just for that one moment of contact.

Though I couldn't yet fix her voice, there was something else I could repair.

When I was sure she was away in her garden, I retrieved a jar from a high shelf. Removing the lid, I looked down into a collection of white glass shards. The decapitated swan head glared at me, blaming me for it being "at loose ends," as it were.

Tipping the pot on the table the white glass tumbled out into a small pile of rubble. It looked pathetic. Bits of doubt crushed in a fit of jealousy. She loved me. I knew it now. Breathing deeply, I held my hands over the pieces and pictured the original in my mind.

My fingers vibrated. My hands trembled. I kept the image firm. The long, slender neck. The wings ready to take flight.

Magic pulsed and poured out of me, encasing the broken pieces in glowing light. The shards levitated off the table and began to spin slowly in the air. Pieces started to form, finding each other and fitting together. A swan was taking shape. It was whole!

Holding it carefully in my hands, I turned it over and sideways, looking for any sign of breakage. There was none. It was just as perfect as the day I first laid eyes on it.

Excitement flooded my heart. This would be the perfect sign that there was hope for her voice! How much more would she love me when I could give her greatest desire?

I carefully put the swan deep in my pocket and ran out to the gardens. I saw her picking green beans. The sun washed over her simple woolen gown. Her straw hat gleamed in the light. I thought what I funny couple we would make—black-haired ghost and a sunny blonde beauty.

My excitement grew almost unbearable as I approached her. Then, I stopped in my tracks.

Marcus, the thorn in my side, stood at her side.

I hid behind a bush and hoped he would leave my darling alone.

"At work so early?" he asked her.

He plucked one of the green beans from her basket and ate it. She smacked him on the shoulder as he grabbed another. The bastard.

Her smile was sweet and infectious all the same. It fled from her lips as he took the basket from her hands and put it down. He slipped his arm around her waist and pulled her toward him. He caressed her cheek and held her chin.

He was going to attack her.

Rage boiled my blood. I made to leap over the hedge and break his neck, but I stopped. My blood turned to ice.

She wasn't terrified. She was grinning. She cupped both his cheeks and pressed herself closer against him. Her hands moved through his hair and caressed his neck. Then, she kissed him deeply.

Every hope in my heart was shattered.

I stumbled backwards, my heart pounding in my ears. It couldn't be possible. I had to be seeing something wrong. But what else could it be?

I wanted to look away, but I could not. I was forced to admire her kiss-swollen lips.

"I can't wait to kiss more of you in a fortnight!" he said roguishly, skittering his fingers under her skirts. "I will do everything in my power to make you the happiest wife in the kingdom."

Wife?

My God!

My stomach twisted in knots and I wanted to vomit. How had I been so blind?

As they embraced again, I knew I was not meant for peace. The magic in my blood would never allow it. Bitterness was to be my destiny, and there was no escaping it. Turning away, I slipped back into the house and the darkness where I belonged.

§

SHE CAME BACK in soon after, smiling and flushed. She placed her basket on the table, turned around, and slapped her hand over her heart at seeing me standing right beside her.

"Is Marcus your fiancé?" I asked icily.

Confusion washed over her. I could almost hear the whispers of her soul. *Did I not know?*

"Are you to be married to that…that man?" I demanded.

She pressed her lips together and nodded warily. I was outraged. She deserved a crown and that man was going to give her nothing but rough hands and an early grave.

"The man is a simpleton," I spat. "You deserve more than a farming life. I can't believe you are willing to accept such meagerness, such mediocrity."

Anger burned bright in her eyes. She grabbed the bucket of beans and spilled them out onto the table. She was trying to tell me she was used to hard work.

"So, you are not afraid of hardship. Well, that's fine. You'd have plenty of that with me as well. Then what is it about him that you don't find in me?"

She studied me gravely, then touched her fingers to her heart and shrugged.

The answer was clear.

"You love him," I said, the words disgusting as they rolled off my tongue. "You don't need a reason. You simply love him."

She nodded.

"That's it then?" I snapped. "You are going to marry a man who offers you nothing when I could offer you a kingdom?"

She stared at me in a silence that was too stubborn to be just natural. I balled my hands into fists to keep the angry magic from escaping. Rage made me strong, and pain made me wild.

"It's very plain now," I snarled. "I see it all. You used me," I seethed.

She shook her head vehemently. The scar rippled across my palm, alive with mad power.

"Once you found I had magic, I was useful to you. Use the monster to get him to fix your broken dishes and mend your birds. Give you a voice so you can say sweet nothings to your lover!" I bellowed.

The magic would be denied no longer. I released it,

blasting the table into splinters, sending the beans flying like a thousand little daggers through the air. Her flame was an inferno, but it wasn't burning for me. It was burning for Marcus…to rescue her.

"What's all this?" Marcus cried, shoving her behind him and rounding on me.

"Ask her," I said, putting all my bile and venom into my smile. "Oh, wait. You can't. Never mind. I'm leaving."

"Get ye gone, beast!" he shouted.

Hate made my magic strong, precise. With a twist of my fingers, I picked him up and slammed him into the wall.

"A beast does as he pleases," I growled, retreating. "You had best remember that."

I took the swan out of my pocket and placed it on the table. It shone brilliantly in the light. Clarice looked down at it in disbelief then up at me, her expression unreadable.

"I would have given you the world," I said quietly. "Now, you must be content with a bit of glass."

I LEFT HER behind, but my bitterness remained. It festered.

Anytime my skin warmed with the memory of her touch, I took a chill from the memory of her perfidy. She had been so kind and warm. She touched me. *Kissed me.* I believed she loved me, but it was all a sick ruse.

I was drowning in resentment. The bile burnt my throat and hardened my heart further than I'd known possible. I was determined it would never be touched again. The man she had found dead on the riverbank had died again. I was what had been reborn, cleansed of weakness and my hunger for revenge returned a hundredfold.

A fortnight passed, and my rage did not ebb. On the contrary, it rose until it crested on the day of their wedding.

Their celebration mocked me, rendered me less than a fool who performed tricks for their amusement. They would soon understand I was not a fool. I was wrath itself.

I approached the village. Trees cracked and split as I walked past. The grass burned in my wake. I chuckled to myself. Marcus thought me a beast. He didn't know half of it.

Music sang through the night chill. The rumble of dancing feet vibrated the cobblestone as I entered the heart of the town. Torches lit up their joy.

I now knew the secret of the magic I had practiced so hard for Clarice. It would not obey love, but it was a slave to hate. Rage was all I needed to wield this wondrous force and make it do terrible and beautiful things. I could make the magic cloak me until I stood in the middle of the revelers, and a snap of my fingers cracked great claps of thunder overhead. I stood before the earsplitting crowd and clapped my hands together.

The slap echoed out causing the ground to quake.

The music died. Their mouths fell silent. All eyes were on me. Fear, not firelight, lit every face now.

The only two who dared stand against the terror of my anger were the happy couple themselves. Clarice and Marcus stood from the garlanded table. I glared at Marcus and cursed my inability to glare at Clarice.

"How dare you show your face here!" Marcus bellowed. "Get out."

"Those not very nice wedding manners," I said, plucking a flower from a woman's hat and sniffing it. "Or, have you forgotten that no one gives orders to a beast?"

Silence.

"Leave," Marcus ground out.

I chuckled.

"Not just yet. You wouldn't have me leave before I give you your wedding gift, would you?" I said. "I only wish to repay everything you *did*."

The flower I held burst into flames. Screams erupted all around, and I felt my lips twist into a devilish smile.

The ground rumbled beneath our feet, the cobblestones roaring as they trembled. Fissures fractured the earth, splitting off like deadly branches, forcing the revelers onto uncertain islands between chasms.

"Stop this madness!" Marcus begged, holding Clarice.

"And short you on what you deserve?" I shot back. "Your reward must be nothing less than exquisite."

I laughed at their terrified faces.

Gurgling up through the cracks in the earth, flames shot up into the night in bright oranges and reds. The black sky was illuminated as the blaze rose high above our heads. The firestorm burned the sky. Burning embers fell onto the guests, singing skin and setting fire to their fine clothes. Screams mixed with the groans of the inferno, creating a fine cacophony the likes of which were usually only heard in the bowels of hell.

It was glorious. Stunning, even.

Marcus now cowered like the dog he was. Through the licking flames, I saw Clarice standing untouched and tall like an ancient statue of some primitive goddess. Her eyes burned me. I knew she finally had seen what I really was.

I fell back, shaking. My shame brought the rain. It doused earth and people alike in cool water. The blaze dwindled until it was nothing but smoldering ash.

Still, one flame remained, the one I had so wanted to appease. Clarice steadily held my gaze as her soul blazed as bright as the sun. The voice of her soul rang out clearly in my head.

Leave and never return.

That was the only wish of hers I could truly ever grant. I bowed my head, feeling the rain drip down my hair and off the tip of my nose. I turned and bled back into the night.

I never looked back.

I never would.

EXCERPT FROM "SPIN: A FAIRY TALE RETELLING" OF RUMPELSTILTSKIN

Laila

After my mother's death, I was at the complete mercy of my father. To put it plainly, he was a drunk, spending what little money our small mill earned on liquor and women instead of food for his family. Forgetting his own pain came at the cost of his child, and I often believed my mother was lucky the plague took her when it did.

Father had another vice that caused me greater fear than being turned out on the streets. He loved to boast, and my heart was crowded with humiliation and anger because of it.

I hated the jackals he attracted to our doors from this dangerous pastime. He would tell of great adventures he never took, discoveries he never made, and of his singular daughter, who possessed talents she never had. It made me ill imagining how he drank in the impressed gazes of the crowd, as his tapestry of lies grew ever thicker.

Now I was one and twenty and working as hard as any man trying to escape the threat of ruin. All I had was the prospect of a fortuitous marriage, but who would have me in this state? Not even Ernis, the fishmonger's son, wanted to make me an offer anymore.

I dragged a full sack of flour across the dirt floor and threw it with the others. The fire behind me snapped and spit, and I ducked just in time to miss the low beams of our sinking home. The walls leaned to the right, and when the wind blew the entire building moaned.

Shaking off the layer of flour from my skin, I looked back at the orders still waiting to be filled. Eight bags, each promising the coins we so desperately needed to survive. My fingers ached, but rest was a luxury I couldn't afford.

Besides, the pain distracted me from thinking of my father's ramblings at the pub. Last year, one of his tales nearly got us arrested. He claimed he killed a king's deer, and that I cooked it into a stew more delicious than the crown's own cook's. Thankfully, I was able to prove our innocence and the gallows were averted. This time.

Moments like that made my black thoughts boil and seethe, though I hated to admit to them. My life was a never-ending series of nightmares thanks to that man. Resentment festered, and in the deepest part of my heart, I secretly wished death would take him, for my sake, but also for his. Maybe then, he would finally be free from his pain.

I was just tying the sack closed when I heard footsteps approaching outside. It was early morning by now, just in time for my father to come home from the pub and sleep off the whiskey. If I were lucky, he would be too drunk to tell me of his conquests...or his lies.

Gravel and dirt crunched beneath his feet in a nerve-wracking rhythm. But as they drew closer, the sound grew into a terrifying, muffled chorus of footsteps, jangling metal, and indistinct shouts.

I dropped the sack and opened the door to see four guards marching towards our mill, a mule following behind them. The mule dragged a small prison wagon, my father its rope-bound cargo. My cheeks flushed with anger and fear.

A rough hand pushed me out of the way as the guards filled the room, the pungent smell of beer, dirt, and horses wafting around them.

"Father! What have you done?" I asked hotly as they dragged him inside, his face ashen as he blubbered nonsense about spinning wheels and gold.

I was stopped by the outstretched arm of a particularly grisly-looking guard with a mesh of scars stretching like a net across his face. An insignia of a lion roaring on his breastplate told me he was not just a simple guard, but their captain.

"This the girl?" the captain demanded of my father, a sneer stretching the scars into a gruesome map as he turned to me. He grabbed my hands and examined them closely.

"I told them! I told them about your spinning, Laila!" Father whimpered. "But they wouldn't believe your gifts otherwise. I couldn't have them thinking I produced a talent-less daughter. I had no choice but to protect my honor."

"You fool!" I cried. Horror rushed like cold water over every muscle of my body. "What have you told them this time? What lies have you spewed out of that foul mouth of yours?"

He only quivered like a common street rat and for the first time in his life was silent. I was on my own to save our lives, just as before with the deer.

"Your presence is required immediately before the king," the captain's voice cut in. "Your father finally revealed the secret you've been keeping hidden from his majesty. You're both lucky if you don't lose your heads for concealing such an extraordinary gift. If you can do half of what we heard, the king is in for quite the surprise."

"I don't have any secrets," I seethed, standing before the

captain. "Whatever he has told you is a delusion. A bit of whiskey and a great deal of madness."

His eyes narrowed and he pointed a callused finger at me.

"That is for the king to decide," he hissed back. "You might be playing the fool with me, but I wouldn't try that little game with his majesty if I were you."

"I would not dare jest about something like this," I pleaded. "Don't you realize my father is out of his mind? Look at him! Look around you. Count the leaks coming in through the roof! We have nothing. Can't you see?"

"Do you really want to know what I see?" the captain snapped. "What I see are either two peasants keeping a secret and preventing the king from what he is owed, or two liars that deserve to be hanged for treason."

His breath stank of ale. Rage ate at me that he insisted on believing my drunken father's drunken lies. Fear made me bold.

"I demand you tell me what secret I am accused of keeping," I stated coldly. "What treason have I committed?"

"*She demands,*" another guard mocked. Laughter erupted all around, its dark, full sound making me feel small—worse, weak and helpless. "For someone who can spin straw into gold, you'd expect she'd be a bit more refined in her manner of speaking."

The sensation of fire seared my lungs and charred my hope as everything became clear.

"Is that truly what this is all about?" I wheezed, pushing the words through my tightening throat. "You think I can spin straw into gold? Surely you know that's not possible! It's only the ravings of a drunk! Father, tell them the truth. Tell them it was only the drink!"

My father gazed glassily at me, his lips stubbornly slack. Every second of silence that followed might as well have been a knife in my back.

The captain laughed deep from his lungs as he patted my father on the shoulder.

"Good lad. For once your father knows when to keep silent," he said. "You, on the other hand, could learn a lesson from him. I have dogs that are trained better than you."

I couldn't control my temper any longer. Before I realized what foolishness I was doing my hand flew out towards his face, but his hand gripped my wrist, stilling my attack. My head snapped back as strong fingers grabbed my hair. The cold bite of a dagger pressed against my neck as the captain seethed.

"Such violence is not becoming of a woman, although it is hard to tell if you even are a woman under such a layer of filth." His men roared with laughter. "I've had enough of your theater. If you say one more word, I swear I will cut out your tongue! You don't need to talk to spin gold for the king. Follow your father's example. I told him if he remained quiet he might stand a chance of survival, and so far he is thriving."

I knew it was useless, even treasonous to fight. Yet, I couldn't help struggling against his grip as he bound my hands with rope. My legs flailed and jerked as I kicked out. I spit in their faces as I tried to pull away again, but their grips only tightened.

I struck one's face with my foot with a resounding, satisfying crack, and his nose spurted blood.

"Make her still!" he exclaimed, wiping the crimson away with his dirty hand.

Pain sliced through my skull like lightning as something hard hit the back of my head. Everything blurred into smears of colors. My legs gave way and I fell to the ground limp and defeated.

"Merick, take her to the prison wagon," a voice ordered as they dragged me outdoors.

My father's voice echoed somewhere in the distance

begging for forgiveness. I saw the lightening sky through black bars and hard wood pressed into my back.

Everything spun, and darkness ate up my incoherent world.

F ind *Spin: A Fairy Tale Retelling (Spindlewind Trilogy Book One)* at a wide selection of online retailers!

THANK YOU!

I sincerely hope you enjoyed reading this book as much as I enjoyed writing it. If you did, I would greatly appreciate a short review on Amazon or your favorite book website, such as Goodreads! Reviews are crucial for any author, and even just a line or two can make a huge difference.

NOVELS

The **_Spindlewind Trilogy_**, a dark fantasy, paranormal romance
retelling of Rumpelstiltskin

Spin

Twist

Break

NOVELLAS

The Crown

A dark retelling of the _Twelve Dancing Princesses_

ABOUT THE AUTHOR

Genevieve Raas is an international bestselling author living in the US with her husband and rather haughty Chihuahua, Mr. Darcy. When she isn't writing dark fairytales or fantasy, you can find her plotting out her next travel destination.

A graduate from Indiana University, Genevieve holds a Master's Degree in English and a Master's Certificate in Professional Editing. She has worked as Lead Transcriber on several published anthologies, including: The Collected Stories of Ray Bradbury, Volume 2 and the New Ray Bradbury Review.

Now, she is venturing out on her own, into the wilds of untamed lands and untold stories.

Genevieve loves connecting with her readers!
www.genevieveraas.com
genevieveraas@genevieveraas.com